Advance Praise for the Book

Iam astounded at Yoogesh's decision to write about mythology. He makes a very skilful attempt to write poems on Greek, Norse, Hindu, Christian, Egyptian, Mesopotamian and Buddhist mythology. Yoogesh also highlights the similarities in the various mythologies. His poems encourage us to connect with mythologies. Kudos to his parents for giving him the freedom to explore. I wish Yoogesh keeps researching and writing and we feel proud that he is part of SSVM.

Dr. Manimekalai Mohan
Founder and Managing Trustee
SSVM Institutions Mettupalayam and Coimbatore

Yoogesh's book of poems successfully covers mythology in a condensed form of 50 poems. It gives an insight into the religious and cultural traditions of the world! Yoogesh seems to have a very natural flair for writing. I wish him immense success in this beautiful journey.

Dr. Vidhya Vinod
CEO, STUDY WORLD Education Holding Ltd.
Dubai International Academic City
Dubai

It amazes me to see Yoogesh's extensive study on mythology at this young age. Each poem gives a crystal-clear explanation in simple words without missing important facts. The title *The Magic of Mythology* itself kindles our imagination and interest. And the book keeps our interest intact, offering a plethora of knowledge on the characters. Wishing Yoogesh more success in future!

Krithika Srikrishna

I feel wonderstruck with the innocent innovation of Yoogesh's poetic recital of the mythological facts. The clarity of capturing the common threads of divergent mythologies in his simple recitation makes his poems unique. I wish Yoogesh's journey in exploring the 'Truths of Life' brings out more of his creative writings.

Dr. Sam Jobin Manohar
Managing Partner Talent Planter

Mythology is an integral part of world civilization. It is a doorway to understanding the earlier humans and their relationship with the world. It seems Yoogesh enjoyed doing the background work for the acrostic poems on Mythology. His book has references of important mythological characters from all over the world that takes us beyond normal situations and characters and feed our intellect. In an increasingly globalized world where children are exposed to multiple cultures, Yoogesh's work provides an insight into the various cultures. I wish Yoogesh success in his literary career!

Ramya Ragupathy
Head-Data Analytics,
Humanitarian OpenStreetMap Team

The Magic of Mythology

A Bouquet of Acrostic Poems
from Ancient Times

P.G. Yoogesh

Acknowledgement

With immense gratitude to the Lord Almighty for blessing me with wonderful parents who have constantly supported and encouraged me to write poems and stories. Their extensive vocabulary and constant willingness to answer my queries kept me on track.

Gratitude to publisher Bharath Parthasarathy, who put his trust in me and agreed to publish my book.

Humble Pranams to my Gurus and mentors for their motivation and blessings.

Contents

Introduction

Magic of Mythology is a vivacious poetry collection depicting famous global mythological characters in a unique acrostic poetry style. This smooth blend of the classical with the contemporary bunch of 50 poems feature the mythologies from all parts of the globe. Enjoy the enigmatic revelations of the various mythologies: Greek (10 poems), Norse (5 poems), Hindu (10 poems), Egyptian (5 poems), Christian (5 poems), Mesopotamian (10 poems) and Buddhist (5 poems). This book will entice all young readers who would cherish the experience of the various mythological revelations in short and sweet poetical form.

With *Magic of Mythology*, Yoogesh took his first steps into the amazing world of writing. A cute bundle of curiosity with great interest in reading since childhood, Yoogesh always had multiple questions waiting to be answered. The pandemic unlocked the desktop for him and therein opened up a wealth of possibilities for exploration beyond his home library. He gradually found himself drawn to world history, mythology and of course gadgets.

As his mother, I have found great joy in helping him transform his writings into blogs ever since he was 7 years old at https://pgyoogesh.blogspot.com

On a recent trip to Mumbai, Yoogesh and his older brother Sharvesh were unable to accompany me. We were all missing each other and so I penned these poems for them:

SHARVESH PG

S - You are my SUNSHINE

H - Will HOLD your hand

A - AND walk beside you

R - All through all your ROLLER COASTER rides

V - Until VICTORY is yours

E - Wake-up with bountiful ENERGY

S - To SERVE the SOCIETY

H - Keep your HEAD high at all times

P - Enjoy with your PEER blissfully

G - And thank GOD for all you have

YOOGESH PG

Y - YOU are the love of my life

O - A highly OPTIMISTIC child

O - Go with an OPEN-MIND

G - GAIN immense knowledge

E - To ELECTRIFY your mind

S - And be SELF-RELIANT to SHINE

H - Aim HIGH at all times

P - Waiting to witness my priceless PRINCE

G - GROWING beyond all barriers

In response Sharvesh wrote back the following:

BHUVANESWARI

B - BEAUTIFUL as the rising sun
H - HEART brimming with gold
U - U gave me life
V - VANQUISHED my negative thoughts
A - AMAZING as the brightest star
N - NEVER ever abandons us
E - ELOQUENT in her speech
S - SOOTHENS our mind
W - WARMING and kindling relations
A - ARTISITIC mind
R - RHYTHMIC soul
I - INTERESTS our lives

And Yoogesh shared this:

TREE

T - THE life giving source
R - READY to taking carbon-dioxide
E - EVERGREEN all around
E - EARTH is cool because of you

I constantly endeavor to engage their young and fertile minds with such exchanges. With the grace of God, one such endeavor has taken the shape of this book that you hold.

We hope that you will enjoy this short anthology of poems, finding it as magical as he did, and bless him forward into his writing journey.

Bhuvaneswari Subramani, 2022

Greek
Mythology

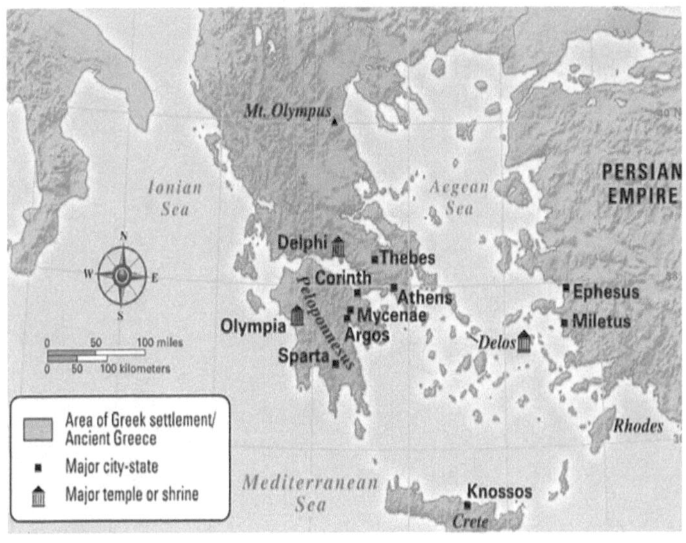

Zeus

Z - Zeus, the last born of Rhea
E - Eileithyia's father
U - Underworld's hater
S - Sun's father

Zeus, the protector of gods
The person who didn't want humans to evolve
The sender of the thunderbolt
To kill evil with a jolt

Poseidon

P - Pegasus's father

O - Oceanus's successor

S - Son of Cronus

E - Eurymede's lover

I - Isthmia, the chief festival in Poseidon's honour

D - Defender of Nereid's honour

O - Odysseus provoker of Poseidon

N - Nereus's son-in-law

Poseidon, father of horses

Creator of the sea's forces

Strike of his trident created springs

To punish Athenians, mighty flood he brings

Hades

H - Hestia's brother

A - Also called Aïdes, the unseen one

D - Destroyer of evil

E - Erinyes's father

S - Stern and pitiless

Hades, the so-called god of evil
Feared by the people
The god of underworld
Determines the life on the world

Hera

H - Hot-headed of all
E - Echo's curser
R - Ruler of the universe
A - Ares' mother

Hera, the queen of gods
Wife and sister of Zeus, the mythical odds
In spite of being goddess of marriage and birth
To be vengeful towards lovers of Zeus is no
     mirth

Hestia

H - Hearth goddess

E - Eleusis' protector

S - Sacrificed the throne

T - Titan Themis' favourite

I - Inversion, eldest and youngest daughter of Titans

A - An immortal who is kind

Hestia kindest of all
Feed the hearth, Hestia shall
Sacrificed the throne
Family's needs above her own

Demeter

D - Deadliest of all

E - Eleusinian Mysteries' central figure

M - Mother of Persephone

E - Demeter Europa, her other name

T - Tomorrow's hope

E - Eleusis her sanctuary

R - Rhea's daughter

Worshipped at Naxos, this underworld divinity

Goddess of health, birth and marriage till
    eternity

Goddess of the field

Always brings her yield

Apollo

A - Also known as Phoebus Apollo

P - Pythia's voice

O - Olympus' brightest

L - Leto's son

L - Litae's brother

O - Oracular god of all

God of archery, music and dance,
Symbol of truth, healing and poetic romance
Slayer of Python
Son of Gaea

Artemis

A - Adonis' hater

R - Raging goddess of all

T - Troy protector

E - Elaphebolia in her honour

M - Mother of virgins

I - Iapetus's son's killer

S - Sister of Apollo

Artemis goddess of forests

Nymphs to watch her dogs while she rests

Moon's goddess assisted her mother

In the delivery of her twin brother

Athena

A - Athena, the friend and slayer of Pallas

T - Troy's enemy

E - Erichthonius of Athens was her adopted son

N - Naxos's protector

A - Ares's bitter enemy

The goddess of wisdom

Protect Athens and is a symbol of freedom

Goddess of handicraft and warfare

Wears a helmet and holds a spear

Ares

A - Ares the killer of many

R - Rage infuser

E - Ethiopia's protector

S - Son of Zeus and Hera

Ares, the god of war

Known for his physical valour

Savage and dangerous with military quality

Sadly personifies sheer bloodlust and brutality

Norse Mythology

Odin

O - Odin the all-knower

D - Dead's recruiter

I - Ireland's favourite god

N - Norse god's king

Associated with wisdom, healing, royalty and
    victory

Also of knowledge, battle, sorcery and poetry

Ancestral figure, Midgard's protector

Ghostly procession of dead has Odin as leader

Thor

T - The most respected god

H - Hildólfr, his brother

O - Odin's son

R - Ragnarök, his death battle

Arch nemesis of Loki, as Thuner

Hammer-wielding god of thunder

Fierce battle with world serpent, Jörmungandr

Odin's human child, immensely popular

Loki

L - Loki the trickster god

O - Odin's enemy

K - Killer of Baldr

I - Ingrateful to the gods

A cunning trickster

Mother of Sleipnir

Husband of Sigyn

Father of monsters, five

Hel

H - Hell's ruler
E - Entity of dishonoured death
L - Loki's daughter

Half-human half dead
Born with evil in head
Hell's embodiment to vie
Destined not to die

Frey

F - Fertility, rain and summer's god
R - Ran's enemy
E - Every body's favourite lord
Y - Ymir's descent

Frey never gets consumed by anger
Rides on a chariot drawn by boar
Abundance to people, a giver
Goddess Freyja's brother

Hindu Mythology

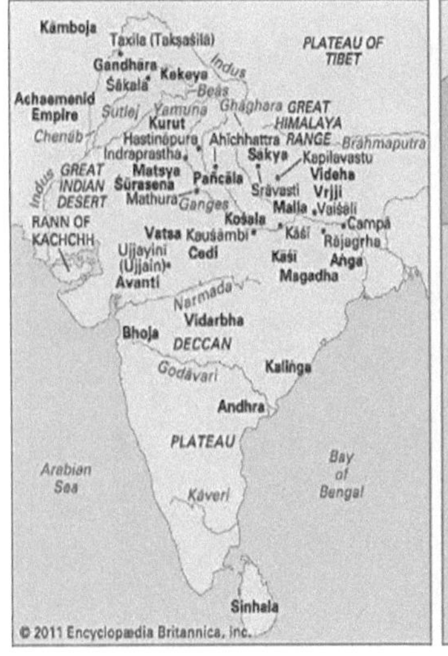

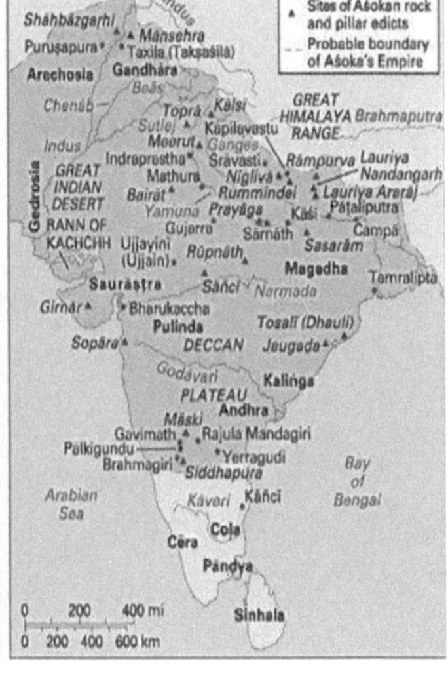
",#

Om

O - Om the sacred symbol
M - Mantras are chanted after it

Om is the supreme mantra
To help attain ultimate reality
Chanted independently or with sincerity
Before any sacred spiritual mantra

Sakthi

S - Sakthi the all-powerful goddess

A - Always kind to good people

K - Kills bad people

T - The creator of the universe

H - Happy are the ones who respect her

I - Is the universal protector

Personification of creative energy

Brings destruction along with synergy

She created the Trimurti and Tridevi

With no beginning and no end, she is Anaadi

Shiva

S - Shiva the omnipresent

H - Hails from Mount Kailash

I - India's most worshipped god

V - Vigilant with third eye

A - Avatars of Shiva are many

Shiva, one of the Holy Trinity
Is father of Ganesha by divinity
The guardian of time
Protector of Vedas, we chime

Vishnu

V - Vaikunta's lord

I - Indra's rescuer after the curse

S - Sathyam, the truth's protector

H - Hindrance to all evils

N - Narayanan's avatars are many

U - Unfair is not in his dictionary

Vishnu, the lord of justice

Preserver and protector of the universe

Helped the world during *pralaya*

Killer of evil Kamsa

Lakshmi

L - Lakshmi the goddess of wealth

A - Alaksmi's sister

K - Krishna's 16,000 wives are her avatars

S - Santana Lakshmi who gives us offspring

H - Her existence gives us the 8 wealth

M - Mahamaya, the goddess of *maya*

I - Incarnation of her is Kalindi

Daughter of the ocean

Lakshmi's incarnation are in thousands

Goddess of beauty, power, fortune, love and
    wealth

Brahma

B - Bhuddi's god

R - Rudra's creator

A - Atri's father

H - Hamsa his *vahana*

M - Mandirs* for him are less

A - Ahimsa is his voice

Brahma, the Vedic god is known as Prajapati

Creator of humans

God of knowledge

His arrogance cost him His fifth head

* Mandir - Temple

Saraswati

S - Saraswati, the goddess of wisdom

A - Avatar of her is Brahmani

R - Righteous in her choices

S - She is a form of Adhiparasakthi

W - Worldly knowledge she possesses

A - Always peaceful

T - Transfers knowledge to those around her

I - Is the all-knowing goddess

She epitomises education, creativity and music
Wife of Brahma
Wisdom and calmness in her attitude
Her blessings make us bow in gratitude

Prithvi

P - Prithvi the goddess of the earth

R - Raging with sadness for her children

T - Tolerant with all happenings on her

H - Helpless against the Asuras

V - Varaha's wife, she is known as Bhumi

I - Is called Ibu Pertiwi in Indonesia

The goddess of nature

Rescued by Vishnu

From drowning

In the ocean of milk

Dyaus

D - Dyaus, the god of the sky

A - Also known as Dyaus Pitar (Father Sky)

Y - You can relate him to Greek Zeus and
Roman Jupiter

U - Uhsas, his daughter, personifies dawn

S - Surya, the son of Dyaus and Prithvi

Dyaus the father of Agni

Dyaus the consort of Prithvi

Dyaus the father of Indra

Ganesha

G - Gana nayaka, the first worshipped god

A - Always loves to eat modak*

N - Not an immortal deity

E - Ever smiling, ever chubby

S - Son of Shiva and Parvathi

H - Hindu god of knowledge, wisdom and
    prosperity

The god of beginnings
Elephant head is his identity
Always kind to others
Superhuman strength and intellectual entity

*Modak - Lord Ganesha's favourite sweet

Christian Mythology

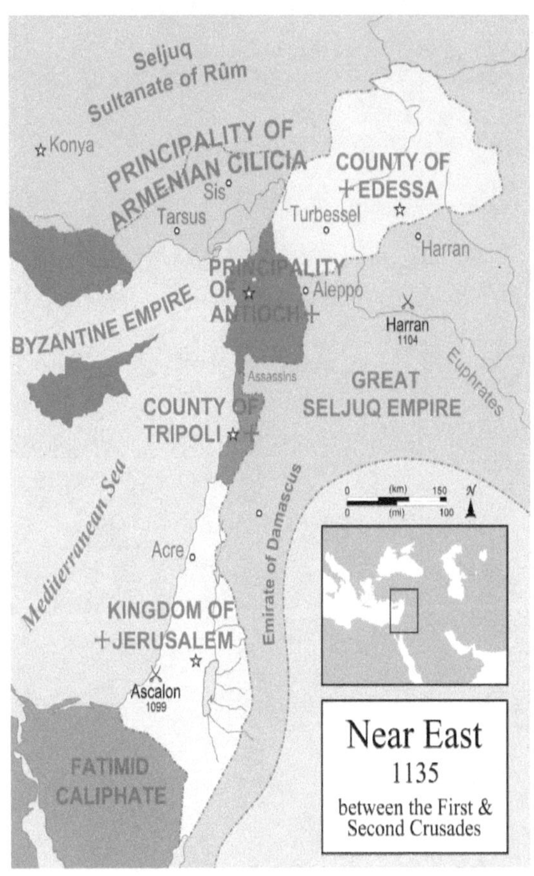

Jesus

J - Jesus the son of god

E - Ever so kind and gentle

S - Smile towards enemies

U - Universe's lord

S - Son of virgin Mary

Jesus of Nazareth, born in Bethlehem

The preacher and leader to the world he came

His birthday, the joyous Christmas day

His crucifixion honoured as Good Friday

Sacrificed his life for sins of men

Rose from death and reached Heaven

M - Mary, the Mother of God

A - After the ascension of Jesus her heart was broken

R - Raised to heaven at the end of life

Y - Your Lord's adorable

She is the mother of Jesus
Wife of Joseph, Queen of Heaven
After death, raised to heaven
Received by Jesus himself

God

G - God the creator of the universe

O - Omnipresent, omnipotent, omniscient

D - Doctrine of the Trinity, creator of the good and bad

The supreme and ultimate reality

The universe's creator

The source of all spirituality

The universal benefactor

Anne

A - Anne, the mother of Virgin Mary

N - Nativity of Mary, ancestor of god

N - Nest of young birds, symbol of Saint Anne

E - Ever so happy and kind

Stands for courage and peace of mind

She is the grandmother of Jesus

Born in Bethlehem in Judaea

Wife of Joachim

Hell

H - Hell is the place for sinners

E - Eternal torment

L - Lucifer's rule

L - Location of evil souls to suffer after death

The place of torture
Fiery, dreaded, painful and harsh
Suffering for unrepentant sinners

Egyptian Mythology

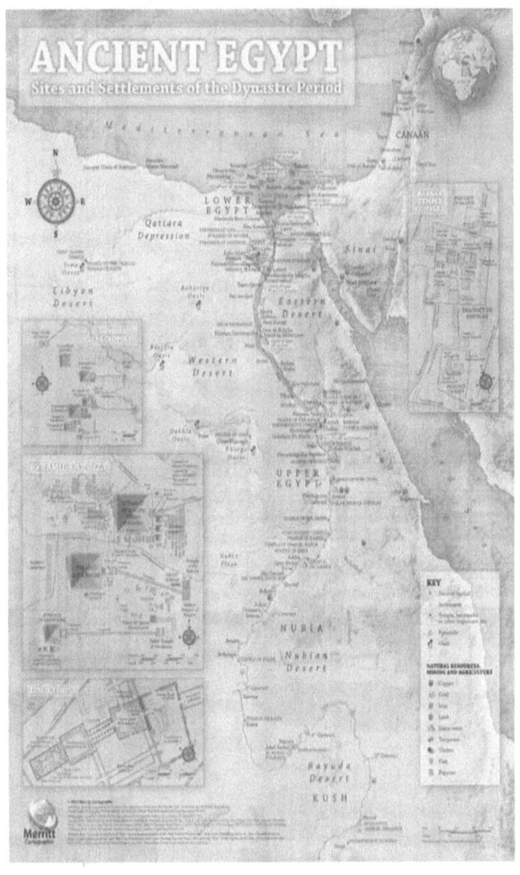

Set

S - Set, the Egyptian god of chaos and war

E - Evil, very strong and dangerous

T - Tornado and sandstorms caused by Him

He was good

But when Ra was dethroned

He became evil

Killed his brother

Took the throne by force

Horus

H - Horus the king of all Egypt

O - One eyed one with falcon head

R - Ra's heir, divine child

U - Underworld king's heir

S - Son of Osiris and Isis

Struggled for 80 years

To become the king of all Egypt!

God of kingship and sky

Under his rule

All of Egypt prospered

Osiris

O - Osiris, the grandson of Ra

S - Silent lord of the underworld

I - Isis's husband

R - Reigning king of the underworld

I - Ipy's son

S - Set's brother

God of order, killed by Seth

God of fertility, resurrected from death

Lord of silence, granted all life

Bears Anubis with Set's wife

Isis

I - Isis, the goddess of knowledge

S - Set's enemy

I - Is the grandmother of Hapy

S - She has the knowledge of 10,000,000 men

The one who dethroned Ra

Helps dead enter afterlife

Saved by Thoth

Replaced by a cow's head

Ra

R - Ra, the first god

A - Apophis's archenemy

Ra the god of Sun

Born from waters of nun

Dethroned by Isis

Replaced by Osiris

Mesopotamian Mythology

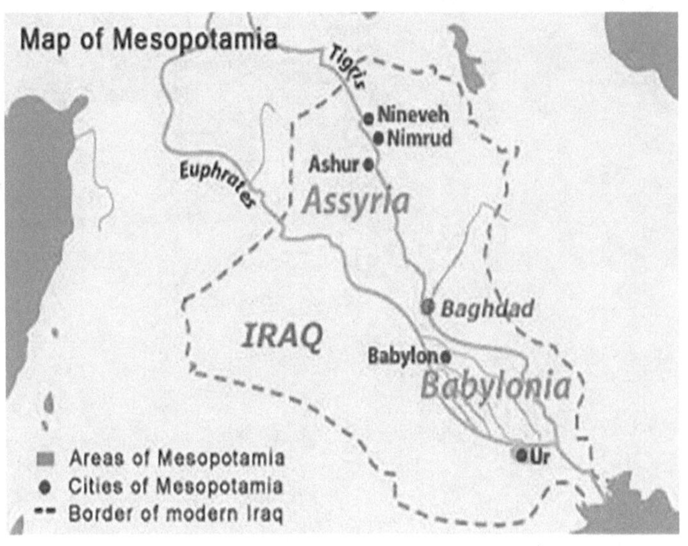

Baal

B - Baal, the god of fertility

A - An equivalent of Zeus

A - An important god of Canaanite

L - Loving and kind to all

Son of Nigal and Suen

The one who has control over the season

Baal, the hero of Baal Cycle of stories

Club-wielding hero with magical weapons

El

E - El the leader of the Canaanite Gods

L - Lord of storm and fertility

Asherah's husband, with grey beard

The status equivalent to Chronos, he shared

Father of gods and good natured

Hadad, Yam and Mot, he fathered

Yam

Y - Yam, the ruler of flood and disaster

A - Also the deity of the primordial chaos

M - Mediterranean sea is his Abode

Yam, one of the Canaanite big three

Rival of Baal

Champion of El

The raging and untamed god of river and sea

Mot

M - Mot the king of the underworld

O - Other gods fear him

T - The equivalent of Hades

The god of death

Not much is known about him

Favourite son of noble El

Yearly gets killed by Anat

Anat

A - Anat, the goddess of love and war

N - Never has taken a wrong step

A - Always supports Baal

T - The queen of gods

H - Hadad's wife

The one who helped
Baal to become the king
She is ruthless in battle
But wise in tactics

A - An, the sky father

N - Never has been disrespected

An the ruler of the universe

Equivalent of Zeus

Ancestor to all Mesopotamian deities

Husband of Ki

Ki

K - Ki, the goddess of the earth

I - Is the sister and wife of An

Equivalent of Gaea

Mother of the Anunnaki

Married her own son

Personification of the earth

Enki

E - Enki the god of the seas
N - Nammu and An's son
K - Ki her wife
I - Is the lord of creation

The god who created the world
Associated with the constellation AŠ-IKU
Father of Marduk
Grandfather of Nabu

Nabu

N - Nabu the god of wisdom

A - A god of literacy and arts

B - Babylon's god's son

U - Universe of knowledge he provides

Patron of scribes* and art of writing

Clay tablet and stylus, Nabu's symbols

Grandson of Enki, his grandfather

Son of Marduk, his father

*Scribes - a record keeper, a person who copies out documents before printing was invented

Utu

U - Utu, the twin brother of Inanna

T - The one who helps Gilgamesh defeat
Humbaba

U - Utu, the sun god

God of justice, morality and truth

Son of An

Father of truth and justice

Rider of the sun chariot

Buddhist Mythology

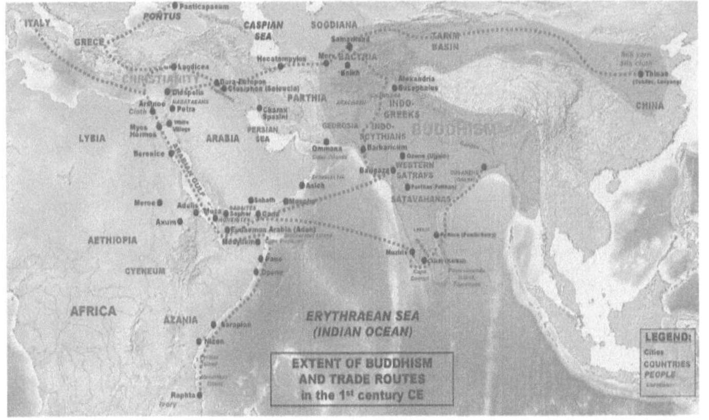

Yama

Y - Yama, the first human to die

A - After lives decider

M - Majjhima Nikaya describes him as a
Vimānapeta

A - Always speaks the truth

Yama, the god of death
Your death decider
If you do good
He will respect you

Buddha

B - Buddha, the selfless one

U - Understanding his teachings is easy

D - Discovered enlightenment under Bodhi tree

D - Dharma's protector

H - He is the one who founded Buddhism

A - Asceticism, self-restraint and meditative
practices

Buddha, the avatar of Vishnu
The awakened one, the enlightened one
The religious leader, preacher and teacher

Rahula

R - Rahula, the son of Buddha

A - A fetter in the path of Buddha's enlightenment

H - His mother is a Arahatà*, Princess Yashodhara

U - Ultimately led to enlightenment by Buddha

L - Lord's son, guarding Buddha's teachings

A - Awaited his birth, spent six years in womb

Rahula, the first and only son of Prince Siddhartha
The successor of Aryadev
Son of Yaśodharā

*Arahatà - A perfected person or someone who has gained knowledge about the true nature of existence and has achieved nirvana or spiritual enlightenment

Ajita

A - Ajita the successor of Gautama Buddha

J - Janama of him is in the line of 10 Buddhas

I - Is the First of the 10 future Buddha's

T - Ten Bodhisattvas, he is the leader

A - Agnidatta, his other name

The heir to legacy of Buddha

The other name is Bodhisattva Maitreya

For 10 Bodhisattvas he is the leader

Always so kind

Tissa

T - Tissa Buddha came to save humankind from pain

I - In Tissa's time, Gautama Buddha ruled Yasavati's men

S - Sujata was then Buddha's name, who became a brahmin

S - Seeing the four sights, he rose from his kingly slumber

A - Ascetics followed him, ten million in number

Tissa, the twentieth Buddha
Like snow melted by heat
Died at Nadarama Monastery
Where his stupa was built
The one who prophesied Gautama Buddha's enlightenment
Lived for 100,000 years, to man's bewilderment

www.ingramcontent.com/pod-product-compliance
Lightning Source LLC
LaVergne TN
LVHW090122180726

843489LV00002B/958